My Science Fair Project

by Judy Kentor Schmauss

HOUGHTON MIFFLIN HARCOURT

PHOTOGRAPHY CREDITS: COVER ©Nicole Hill/Rubberball Productions/Getty Images; 3 (b) ©Nicole Hill/Rubberball Productions/Getty Images; 4 (b) ©Andy Z./Shutterstock; 5 (br) ©David Lade/Shutterstock; 6 (b) ©Corbis; 7 (r) ©Stephen Orsillo/Shutterstock; 11 (br) ©David Lade/Shutterstock

Copyright © by Houghton Mifflin Harcourt Publishing Company

All rights reserved. No part of this work may be reproduced or transmitted in any form or by any means, electronic or mechanical, including photocopying or recording, or by any information storage and retrieval system, without the prior written permission of the copyright owner unless such copying is expressly permitted by federal copyright law. Requests for permission to make copies of any part of the work should be addressed to Houghton Mifflin Harcourt Publishing Company, Attn: Contracts, Copyrights, and Licensing, 9400 Southpark Center Loop, Orlando, Florida 32819-8647.

Printed in Mexico

ISBN: 978-0-544-07265-7

5 6 7 8 0908 20 19 18 17 16

4500607998   A B C D E F G

If you have received these materials as examination copies free of charge, Houghton Mifflin Harcourt Publishing Company retains title to the materials and they may not be resold. Resale of examination copies is strictly prohibited.

Possession of this publication in print format does not entitle users to convert this publication, or any portion of it, into electronic format.

Contents

Introduction 3
Choosing a Project 4
Making a Hypothesis 5
Choosing the Plants 6
Changing the Conditions 7
Observations 8
Conclusions 10
Responding 12

Vocabulary
survive
basic needs
nutrients

Stretch Vocabulary
thrive   consistently
varieties   deficient

Introduction

My name is Taylor. This year, I have decided to enter the school's science fair. I like science, and I thought it would be a fun thing to do.

To enter a science fair, you have to think like a scientist. You have to have a question you want an answer to. You have to have a hypothesis, or a statement that you want to test. You have to investigate and record your results. Then you have to figure out what your results mean.

I cannot wait to get started!

Science fairs are usually held once a year. Children put a lot of work into their projects.

Choosing a Project

My mom tries to grow plants. Some of the plants thrive, or do well, but most do not. Our house has a lot of trees around it, so we do not get much sun. I think that is why her plants do not always survive. Why am I telling you this? I have decided to do my science fair project about plants and sunlight. Here is the question I want to answer: "What happens when a plant gets no sunlight?"

I am not sure what the answer is, so I will investigate.

The plants in Taylor's yard get very little direct sunlight.

Making a Hypothesis

Now I want to make a hypothesis. As you know, a hypothesis is a statement I can test. I will make a hypothesis about what the answer to my question is.

I know that all living things have basic needs. Humans need food, water, air, and shelter. Plants are living things, so they must have needs, too. Is sunlight one of those needs? I am going to say "yes" based on what I have observed about the plants my mom tries to grow. So here is my hypothesis: Plants that get no sunlight will die. Now I have to test it.

How will Taylor support the hypothesis?

Choosing the Plants

I go to the nursery, or plant store, to look at plants. I need two sets of plants: one to put out in the sun, and one to keep in the dark. There are many varieties to choose from. But I need to make sure all the plants I get are the same kind. I choose six of the same variety. I know the plants are not exactly the same in every way, but they have to be as close to the same as possible. I pick six that are about the same height. They are all bushy and healthy.

I bring the plants home. I am ready to start!

What might happen if Taylor chose plants that needed different amounts of sun?

Changing the Conditions

When I get home, I choose two locations for my plants. I put three plants on our back step because it is one of the only places in my yard that gets some sun during the day. The instructions that came with the plants say that they need "part sun, part shade." I think I have chosen a good spot.

I put the other three plants in a closet. It is dark in there. I decide that since I am investigating only the lack of sunlight on a plant, I should keep watering it.

If you are investigating how no water AND no sunlight affect a plant, then you would not water the plant, either.

Observations

For the next seven days, I observe the plants. I decide to look at the plants at the same time each day. At that time, I will water them if the soil is dry. I make a chart. I will write down what I notice about each of the plants each time I look at them. At the end of seven days, I hope I will have the answer to my question.

Here is what part of my chart looks like.

	Plant 1 (with sunlight)	Plant 2 (no sunlight)
Day 1, 6 pm		
Day 2, 6 pm		
Day 3, 6 pm		
Day 4, 6 pm		
Day 5, 6 pm		
Day 6, 6 pm		
Day 7, 6 pm		

It is important to record your observations consistently every day.

The week has gone by quickly. I just recorded the last notes on my chart. I have all the information I need. Take a look.

	Plant 1 (with sunlight)	Plant 2 (no sunlight)
Day 1, 6 pm	stems straight up; leaves flat and green	stems straight up; leaves flat and green
Day 2, 6 pm	stems straight up; leaves starting to point to sun	stems and leaves a bit droopy
Day 3, 6 pm	no change	stems and leaves droopy; 3 leaves getting brown
Day 4, 6 pm	leaves all pointing to sun; stems straight up	10 leaves beginning to get brown; 3 leaves really brown
Day 5, 6 pm	3 new leaf buds	stems bent over; 13 leaves turning brown; 10 leaves fell off
Day 6, 6 pm	3 leaf buds opening; 3 more leaf buds appear	10 more leaves fell off; other leaves stiff and drying
Day 7, 6 pm	flower bud appears; new leaves	all leaves fell off; stem brown, dry, and bent over

Conclusions

All of the plants in the closet died. The results of my test support my hypothesis that plants that get no sunlight will die. Since the plants outside are still healthy, I have concluded that the plants in the closet died because they did not get enough sunlight. Now I have another question: "Why do they need sunlight?"

I look on the Internet and at books in my school library. I find out that plants need nutrients to grow. Nutrients come from the soil. I also find out that plants need water and air. They use sunlight to turn water and air into food. Then I remember that different plants need different amounts of sunlight. That is why the plants are marked differently at the nursery.

So now I know why the plants in the closet died. Since the closet was deficient, or lacking, in sunlight, the plants were not able to make food for themselves. The plants needed sunlight as well as water, air, and soil to survive.

Now I know why my mom's plants do not grow well. She needs to buy plants that do not need a lot of sunlight.

I think that when I win my science fair medal, I will buy my mom a new plant!

Responding

Draw Your Observations

Use the information in Taylor's chart. Draw seven different pictures of a plant, one for each day. Show what happened to it as each day passed. Share your drawings with a friend.

Write About Photosynthesis

Photosynthesis is the process by which a plant uses sunlight to make food. Research photosynthesis and write a report about it. Include a drawing that illustrates how photosynthesis works.